Charles Fletcher Dole

Luxury and sacrifice

Charles Fletcher Dole

Luxury and sacrifice

ISBN/EAN: 9783337305949

Printed in Europe, USA, Canada, Australia, Japan

Cover: Foto ©Andreas Hilbeck / pixelio.de

More available books at **www.hansebooks.com**

LUXURY AND SACRIFICE

BY

CHARLES F. DOLE

AUTHOR OF " THE COMING PEOPLE," " THE GOLDEN RULE IN
BUSINESS," " THE AMERICAN CITIZEN," ETC.

FOURTH THOUSAND

NEW YORK : 46 EAST FOURTEENTH STREET

THOMAS Y. CROWELL & COMPANY

BOSTON : 100 PURCHASE STREET

C. J. PETERS & SON, TYPOGRAPHERS,
BOSTON.

TO

My Helpful Wife,

AND WITH HER TO THE MULTITUDE OF GOOD WOMEN
WHOSE GROWING AND INTELLIGENT INTEREST
IN ALL MORAL, SOCIAL, AND RELIGIOUS
QUESTIONS
IS THE BRIGHTEST AUGURY OF BETTER DAYS FOR
OUR WORLD,

This Little Volume

IS GRATEFULLY DEDICATED.

Whatever noble women pray for,
The men are pledged to do.

INTRODUCTION.

Out of the noisy disputes and sectarian wranglings of many centuries, certain great and simple principles shine forth with growing distinctness. They are peculiarly associated with the name of Christianity, and with the remarkable personality of its founder. Jesus stood for the "Real Presence" of God in this world, as the source of its life; he demonstrated that men might live in union or harmony, not only with one another, but with God; he taught that the life of love, or good-will, is the realization and perfection of manhood; he threw a new meaning into the Golden Rule, and made' it the standard and the bond of human society; by his own life and death he established the marvellous doctrine that the good man, being the child of God, may transform all evil into good, and, having borne toil, suffering, and pain, may develop stronger faith, warmer love, more ardent hope, and abounding life.

These principles have never as yet been broadly applied, or reduced to common practice. They have never been even understood by any considerable number of so-called Christians. A conventional or ceremonial religion, consisting of certain external acts, or involved in various rather metaphysical dogmas, has in various forms largely taken the place of the beautiful ethical and spiritual religion that inspired Jesus, lifted his humble followers to a new level of courage and serene happiness, and glowed in the earnest devotion and eloquence of Paul.

The early religious teachers were like men who, we

may suppose, had discovered the secret of the power of steam, and had begun to apply it in the days of the Pharaohs. But the world was not ready for their great invention; human industry was not well enough organized to take it up; slavery and other barbarisms stood in its way; "the age of steel" was still in the future. So the world failed to perceive Jesus' secret of life. Men's minds were still full of prejudices and superstitions. The early Christianity was confused with the strange notions of the times. There was neither science nor philosophy mature enough to co-operate with the religion of the beneficent God and the Golden Rule.

The new religion appeared at first as an element of antagonism in the world. To the minds of primitive men a vast dualism seemed to offer itself, both in nature and in all human conduct. Christianity came into the world to wage war on evil. "The world, the flesh, and the devil" was the evil trinity against which the sons and daughters of God were called to contend. Real life was rather to be expected in another existence than actually to be found here. This earth at its best was a school of probation. With such a conception of the earthly life, the attitude of the Christian before the practical problems of civilization was naturally that of suspicion and hostility.

The processes of ancient civilization, the slave-system of industry, the art and the music, the theatre and the arena, the literature, the government, in the world of the Cæsars, could hardly have been recognized by the plain Christian as in any sense the movement of ideal and spiritual forces. The civilization of Rome and Byzantium was, in his eyes, a colossal display of the allurements and temptations of the Evil One.

The noblest and most religious minds stand to-day in a new attitude with regard to the problems of civilization. While we recognize the animalism and barbarism in our world, we proceed to our tasks without a fear or even a haunting thought of the presence of a devil. We have ceased to think of our senses or our bodies as enemies lurking to betray us; we hold them to be our servants to command. We say, "All good things are ours, nor soul helps flesh more now than flesh helps soul." This is to believe that the world is God's world. Our work is not to fight it, so much as to control and use it. This involves a new application of the principles of religion. It is nothing less than to win over to the acknowledged area of beneficence and human service all the complex processes of civilization, — the arts and industries, literature and the drama, amusements and recreation. It is also to enter the realm of politics, and to pervade all the functions of the state with a wise and righteous friendliness. The government must be made the expression of the organized good-will of the people. We are fairly beginning to see that we have in Christianity, in the broadest and most universal sense of the word, a force capable of harmonizing and bringing into unity all the diverse elements both of individual and of social life.

It is my wish in this little book to illustrate the practical working of our fundamental religious principles, with respect to the important and difficult problem of luxury. If it is possible to render the use of luxury beneficent, there is nothing that we cannot likewise convert into the means of human welfare.

I am aware that luxury is to a considerable extent at present the result of the inequality in men's industrial and social condition. It is involved with the existence of private property. The abolition of all private property, however, if this were wise and right, would not, as we shall see, remove luxury from the world. The question would still arise, how it should be distributed and controlled. I shall assume here that, at least for a long time to come, we must contemplate more or less inequality of human condition. This is true, whether we like it or not. Among all the plans for social improvement before the world, there is none that opens any practicable way for lifting millions of mankind, or even the millions of the most favored country of the world, immediately to a uniformity of outward condition. It is not merely true that some now are allowed to hold more than others; the services of some are socially far more precious than the services of others; moreover, the needs of some are much greater than the needs of others. The skilled scientific investigator, or the gifted singer, like Patti, for instance, requires much more of the world than the average farm laborer. So far, then, as the existence of luxury is dependent upon inequality of income, we are obliged to face this as a fact that may indeed be considerably modified, but cannot be abolished altogether. Our problem is nothing less than the practical application of the highest teachings of our religion to existing facts. Can the good and true man, the man who honestly loves his fellows, safely and generously use and handle luxury? If so, how can he do this without growing idle and selfish? And, finally, how shall we actually combine the free use of the growing wealth of the world with the great ancient and profound thought of sacrifice, without which religion itself would cease to hold earnest men's respect?

LUXURY AND SACRIFICE.

I.

THE GROWING
TIDE OF
LUXURY.
THE righteous handling of luxury is a
subject that has baffled earnest minds since
men began to think. What is luxury? It
is not easy exactly to define it. The luxuries of one age
have often become the mere comforts, or even necessities,
of a later generation. Window-glass, for example, once
a costly symbol of wealth, and the subject of special
taxation, is now found everywhere except among half-
civilized peoples. The vast middle class in England and
America are doubtless better housed and clothed and fed
than the aristocrats of the fourteenth century.

Moreover, the people of the same community do not
agree as to what constitutes luxury. To many plenty
of domestic service would appear to be luxury; to others
ample service seems to be a daily necessity, without
which life would hardly be worth living.

In a large way, however, we all know quite well what
we mean by luxuries. We mean grand houses, costly
furniture, private libraries, paintings and statues; elegant dinners, with many courses, flowers, and beautiful
table-ware and plate; yachts and horses and carriages;
theatre and opera tickets, and the best concerts; rich
dress, silks and lace, gold, jewels, and ornaments. We
may include also the advantages of thorough education

and culture, with free opportunity to travel at home and abroad.

The average American household probably has not six hundred dollars a year. The man's tobacco and beer, the woman's cup of tea, an occasional holiday in the public park, a cheap seat at the theatre, — such things as these are the luxuries of multitudes. By comparison the favored minority, who spend incomes of thousands of dollars a year, may be said to constitute a luxurious class.

What must thoughtful and humane men say of all this vast and growing tide of luxury? There is a distinctly narrow answer to this question, to which our sympathies often incline us. As we see the splendid palaces in a great city, New York or Paris or London, the lavish entertainments, banquets, balls, and weddings, the display and pomp, the liveries and equipages, and then visit the squalid tenement-houses only a few blocks away, where the poor are crowded by thousands, the contrast seems too terrible to contemplate. Here are women earning by toilsome days less, we are told, than a dollar a week. Here are children brought up to the constant sight of vice. Grant that multitudes get something of net gain out of this burdensome struggle; grant that human nature, in its genuine qualities of virtue, fidelity, and heroism, asserts itself often splendidly amid the most dismal surroundings; grant that the roots of human happiness are quite independent of circumstances, and that the good God bids little children play as joyously in dingy alleys as in a nobleman's park; grant also that our grand system of public schools is surely working to lift the standard of life in every dark corner of a city: nevertheless, the stern question forces itself upon us; what right have any set of men or women to pour out expense on their own enjoyments, to eat and drink the wealth of the world, while just around the corner colossal needs call for relief, and wrongs go unredressed? What right have people who worship on Sunday in the richly upholstered pews of elegant churches to call themselves "Christians," the disciples of the greatest friend of the poor, a poor man himself, whose gospel was a doctrine of brotherhood, while the poor do not appear and scarcely are welcome in the same luxurious churches?

Is it surprising that some are tempted in their mingled indignation and sympathy to cry out against all this show of luxury as unseemly and evil? Is it strange if many who look on are angry and bitter, and threaten social revolution? Let men first minister with their money to actual human necessities, and let them at least postpone their self-indulgences while the cry of the poor is so loud.

The free enjoyment of luxury not only seems to be a wrong to the poor, who need the very things — decent houses, wholesome food, education — which the money expended in extravagance might purchase for them; the use of luxury is also claimed to be most demoralizing to the luxurious class, and especially to their children. It was said of the young men of the wealthy set in a New England town, that only one of them escaped "as by fire" from the grim fate of worthlessness, insanity, or early death that pursued them all. Every one has heard of similar groups of young men, representing "the best families." We all know that the worst possible education for a child is to be brought up to be idle, to be waited upon, and to have plenty of money to spend.

So much for the revulsion of feeling with which, in view of the extreme facts of the contrast between wealth and poverty, we are tempted to turn against luxury. We are almost persuaded to revolt against an order of society that permits luxury. Our sympathies range us, for the moment at least, with the austere and ascetic Savonarolas — the opponents of all mundane pleasure. We feel rebuked for the selfishness with which we may have set our eyes on the pomps and vanities of the world.

Who are the good and wise ascetics, however, to solve the problems of practical duty which they so easily raise? Who that decries luxury in general is consistent enough to have no use for it himself? Who will draw the nice line that separates the good and true man's necessities — his immaculate linen, his open fireplace, his books and pictures — from mere vain self-indulgence? The truth is, no Puritan majority can vote the fact of luxury out of the world. On the contrary, it seems to be a necessary element of life. Like all other elements, it is not to be summarily condemned because some men have too much of it. It may, indeed, be likened to the adipose tissue of the body. The well-made body does not consist merely of bones and muscles and brain; there is health in plump and ruddy cheeks, and a certain proportion of fat in the system. True human life likewise insists upon keeping all the materials with which we are set to construct the temple of civilization. As we learn to find new uses for the waste and by-products of our mills and mines, and as we thus add material wealth to the common store, so out of all the materials of human life we are set to learn the higher uses, and to convert what was once " waste " into worth and value.

II

THE APOLO-GISTS FOR LUXURY.   Let us frankly face certain claims that the friends and defenders of the luxuries are sure to make. These claims may not at first appeal to our sympathies, but they are very interesting; they involve profoundly humane considerations, they have reason in them, and they are as needful to our full understanding of the subject as are the just complaints from the other side.

In the first place, we are reminded that the poor would be the last to ask us to banish luxury from their sight. Why do men so strongly desire to live in the great cities? It is because they love to see the show, the display, the grand windows full of beautiful things, the ceaseless procession of wealth, the magnificent buildings. It is doubtful if the poorest half of the population of New York would vote to-day to tax out of existence the gorgeous turnouts in Fifth Avenue, or the steam yachts on the bay. Who will say that the very poor in London would not vote to keep royalty and the House of Lords?

Moreover, as we have seen, the poor have their own relative luxuries. We suspect that they pay more heavily than the rich for their luxuries, and bear, therefore, a more severe weight of taxation. Their dream and their hope is that they or their children may one day ride also in carriages, and dine in elegant club-houses. This may be an unworthy and material dream, we may condemn it as contrary to the ideal of true human progress. But multitudes cherish such dreams as this. They do not wish to abolish luxuries; they wish to bring them within their reach, they wish to enjoy them.

We are brought at once to a great economic claim in behalf of luxury.   Luxury, we are told, is the prize of efficient and successful effort.   Give the worker enough surplus of earnings to be able to buy a treat for himself, — a Sunday dinner, or a drive into the country, — and he will put the energy of hope into his labor.   The boy from the farm or the little village among the hills sees in the great houses, the display, and the liveries, the sumptuous entertainments, so many glittering prizes, to stir his ambition.   Here is the stimulus of inventive and organizing genius.   Thousands of men struggle for the prize, and put forth all their activity.   Meantime, out of their myriad efforts, vast factories rise, new and more perfect machinery is set to work, power is brought out of the depths of the earth, systems of industry are co-ordinated and economized, the wheat-fields of Dakota are turned into garden-spots for New York and London, the Old World nightmare of famine becomes a mere detail of history.   Lo! out of this ceaseless pursuit of the prizes of luxury, the poor are better fed and housed and clothed.   Grant that the grand dividend of the labor of the world is not yet fairly distributed.   Nevertheless, as a rule, all work harder, almost necessarily produce more, and on the whole actually receive more, because there are splendid prizes to which men lift up their eyes, and which a few men are seen actually to win.   Would these captains of industry, these inventors, these promoters of gigantic corporations, work so hard and conquer such arduous undertakings, if they saw at the end of the race nothing more substantial than Mr. Bellamy's proposed decorations of honor, or if they had to content themselves with the inward satisfaction of duty well performed?   Those of us who believe most fully in the divine possibilities of our common manhood can at least easily forgive those who doubt whether men are either intelligent or good enough as yet to dispense with the tangible prizes of effort. Surely one way in which men learn the higher values of life is through habits of self-control gained by handling for themselves the material values. The good things of life are like the counters by the use of which the children learn numbers. The gospel of progress for a childish people, like the blacks in the South, may lie in the quite prosaic industrial duty of getting money and houses and lands. The grander doctrine of the co-operative commonwealth rises out of discipline learned through the winning and the possession of individual wealth. May there not be an important truth here for all our social reformers?

The defenders of luxury make a further claim. They show us that the pomp and the flaunting banners of wealth are the symbols that lead the march of true civ-ilization. As the athletic group in a university, while often overdoing physical exercise, exaggerating its rela-tive value, and making themselves ridiculous by their one-sided devotion to it, yet set the pace for all their fellow-students, arouse and maintain a wholesome in-terest in manly sports, and raise the average of health for thousands of young men; so in a different way the luxurious class, though with serious loss to their own best development, with the sacrifice of happiness, with real injury to their children through their exaggeration and excess, yet mark the way where the many are bet-ter and happier for following. The average demand for all that makes civilization is increased. Because the rich live in palaces, multitudes, imitating them at a safe distance, possess ampler houses. Because the rich have lawns, parks, and greenhouses, the poor take the more pains to keep their streets clean, and flowers are seen in every window. The wealthy buy costly paintings, and straightway the same paintings are reproduced for the millions. The rich man's carriage becomes the model after which railway cars are built for all men to ride in. Already certain modern States and cities lay out forests and public gardens on a scale with which princes can hardly compete, while the municipal libraries and art museums outstrip the grandest private collections. Thus the few take the lead, investigate and experiment with the good things of the world; and the multitude, following after, reap the advantage. It may even be claimed, that in numerous instances, the many would not have known what was good, if the few had not first made the discovery, and set the new fashion, and so instituted the demand on which the larger supply speedily follows. Thus the whole world grows rich in the appliances of civilization.

One more ingenious claim is made on account of the benefit that the luxurious class confers upon the poor. Whatever the rich spend, even for the most extravagant and useless entertainment and display, must be distributed in some form in wages to the poor. An army of people have constant maintenance in the service of the wealthy. In other words, luxury makes an enormous increase of labor and employment. Cut off all the cost of grand dinners and greenhouse flowers, of fancy balls, gorgeous dress, and jewels, of horses and yachts, and you would cut off the living of more people than you imagine.

Perhaps this consideration hardly bears careful scrutiny. If waste and extravagance distribute wages and furnish employment, so also do fire and shipwreck and war. Is it a good thing to eat and drink ten thousand dollars worth of human labor in a single half-barbaric feast? Why is it not also a good thing that a house burns down, and likewise distributes the insurance money among men who need work?

It must be confessed that waste is waste, whatever be the form in which the results of men's toil are consumed. Let self-indulgence be frank with itself, and not profess to urge as its justification the love of the poor, or the desire to distribute its money in charity. If the rich man wishes to spend wages in building a palace, he is not confined to the necessity of building for his own ostentation. However he employs his money, whether he spends or invests it, he must distribute it. The lavish use of costly wines distributes money. The erection of improved working-men's cottages distributes money. But the one use may waste like a fire, while the other stores up good for generations.

There is, however, a measure of truth in the claim that the rich accidentally help the poor, even by the very excess of their luxuries. We do not yet know how to use all the surplus labor of the nation. We do not produce any less wheat or cotton cloth because of the army of labor that waits upon the luxuries of the rich. It is better to have all these employed, though their labor results in little permanent value to the life of the nation, than it would be to keep them in idleness. By and by we may learn to employ the labor of the world more economically; but till we learn to do so better than now, it is probable that the sum of the productive labor of the world is not less, but a little more, on account of the demands made in behalf of luxury. If this is true, it needs to be also clearly stated that it is a confession of weakness and the want of real civilization. It is no reason why we should not try to find better, saner, and more humane methods of employing labor.

III.

WHAT ARE LUXURIES? Mere economical considerations soon weary us. We need to lift up our eyes to the hills and the stars, and so to raise our problem to the range of ethical and humane principles.

There is one general characteristic that describes all luxuries. A luxury is that of which "there is not enough to go around," as we say. The supply is limited. Either only a few can possess it at all, as, for instance, a beautiful painting, or if it is a thing which many can enjoy, there is a limitation upon their use of it. They must take turns in enjoying it; or they must exercise a certain self-restraint, or else do a wrong to others. The luxury is that of which there is not enough for every one to use all the time, or as much as he pleases.

The luxury thus has the quality of an exceptional enjoyment. A simple illustration is in the case of the little stock of jellies and preserves which the frugal country housewife used to store away for the year. There was not enough of these preserves for use every day. There was not enough, when the special treat was brought on, for every schoolboy to help himself to as much as he pleased. The very limited supply made the preserves a luxury.

It is obvious that this limited and exceptional character of the luxury ought not to debar its use. Here is a good thing, not, therefore, to be thrown away because it is an exceptional good. Those who must go without are no worse off because some possess it. Not all men can live on the corner lot, or on the crown of the hill. Not all women can wear diamonds, or possess ancestral furniture brought over in the Mayflower. It is good to have the rare book in the public library, even if some one who wants to read it has to wait a long time, or does not draw it at all. With respect to a considerable class of good things, those of us who do not have them are at least no poorer because certain more fortunate persons possess them. These others do not necessarily possess them at our loss. If we cannot have them, we should cheerfully vote that some one should get the benefit of them. The world is richer so.

Luxuries in this respect may be likened to certain special gifts of beauty, talent, skill, or genius. There are only a few really beautiful persons in a town; there are only a few men of genius in a century; high skill is not very abundant. But all of us who are common men and women would gladly choose to see men and women among us more gifted than we are. We are all richer and better for their existence. So we say with regard to the luxuries. Whatever is good we wish to keep in the world. If we cannot have it for ourselves, we are glad that some other man has it. The luxuries are here to be possessed, handled, and enjoyed. Out of a better use and enjoyment of them we are to win a nobler human development.

We are ready now to discern the principle in the light of which luxuries must henceforth be considered and administered. Here is a class of enjoyments that are more or less exceptional and limited. Not all can have them; but the few are herein lifted, at least for the moment, upon the toiling shoulders of the many. If we could think of men as only animals, or slaves, or machines, this fact might have no special significance. But as soon as we realize that men are brothers, of one blood and one nature, the fact that the many are without that which some of us possess, or are at work while we are enjoying ourselves, gives our pleasure a quality that may truly be described as sacred.

The story is told that when King David was beleaguered by the Philistines close to the home of his boyhood, weary and thirsty, he sighed for water from the well by the gate in Bethlehem. The well was in the hands of the enemy; and his mighty men, at the risk of their lives, broke through the lines, drew water from the well, and brought it to the king. The king could not think that this was mere ordinary water. It was equivalent to the blood of brave men. He would not even drink it himself, but poured it out as a libation to God. This story is a parable to illustrate the sacred character of luxury.

Luxury represents more or less the labor, the risk, the sacrifice, perhaps even the life, of men. As a rule it has been bought with human toil. It may be foolish, like David, to pour out the precious water on the ground; but it is at least fair, humane, and truthful for the man who enjoys an income of ten thousand dollars a year to reflect upon what it means to have control over as much as the sum of the work of twenty average laborers! Surely that is sacred which the one only may have, while the many may be suffering real want.

Sometimes the luxury bears an obviously sacramental quality. The frugal housewife did not put up her jellies for the strong and well, but with kindly forethought for the sick, the aged, and the convalescent, or as her compliment to an occasional guest, or for the rare joy of the family reunion at Thanksgiving time. The valid justification for many a luxury, like the woman's alabaster box of ointment in the story of Jesus, is that it is a pure sacrifice for love's sake. To accept or to use it in greed or selfishness would be a species of sacrilege.

The nation sets its chief magistrate in the White House, and surrounds him with a certain magnificence. It is in the same spirit, and with the same significance, as when, in old times, they consecrated a king. The President does not belong to himself, but to the people, of the United States. The generous service, the flowers, and the ample rooms of the White House represent the good-will and the dignity of the people. A shame on the magistrate, high or low, who does not see that his place and belongings, his salary and emoluments, are sacred to the people who give them.

IV.

NOBLESSE OBLIGE. We come at once to the sight of certain simple conditions that govern the use of the luxuries. The first condition is modesty. A shallow mind might indeed interpret the fact of his being lifted above the heads of his fellows to some rare sight of enjoyment, into the terms of pride and egotism. "See me," the vain man might cry out; "behold I am greater and higher than others!" Surely no true man, reading the facts of life, can harbor such conceit. "Who am I," says the just man, "that I should be surrounded with beautiful things, that I should possess abundance of power, that the opportunities of the world should be open before me? Do I deserve gratifications which multitudes never begin to realize?" In a world where the noblest and best have often had to go hungry and to suffer, and the cross has been the symbol of goodness, how can any man dare to give the free rein to easy indulgence?

Truthfulness and modesty, in fact, serve to steer a man away from all excess in luxury. The modest man would not wish to build himself a palace, even if he could afford the expense. He does not believe that a palace fits the state of the private citizen. The modest man, however rich, does not desire pomp and display around him. He cannot bear that the sight of his entertainments shall make a Lazarus at his door envious and bitter, or that the splendor of his equipage or his yacht shall mark the contrast of the squalor of tenement-houses. Modesty sees no fitness in show and extravagance. Intelligence discerns in many a modern metropolis merely the glittering survival of barbaric egotism.

A second consideration that impresses every one who, while enjoying his luxuries, sees in them the sacred element of human cost, is the duty of increased efficiency which their cost commands. Does the great world, in whatever mysterious, haphazard manner, pick me out of the millions, and let me ride in a carriage and sail in a grand steam-yacht? Does it send me to the seashore or to the mountains for my vacation? Does it allow me to travel like a prince around the world, to see beautiful cities, their museums and their masterworks of art and genius, to make the acquaintance of notable men, to behold stupendous Alpine or Himalayan scenery? Here is a solemn bond imposed upon me, to be a man worthy of all this splendid expenditure. God forbid that I should have the face to enjoy and absorb, and to give nothing back. God forbid, if the world asks any service of me, that I should be so mean as to refuse. Show me rather what I can do to repay the world and mankind for what I have consumed.

Suppose, again, that I am one out of the thousand to whom the prize of a university education has fallen. While the multitude were bending at their toil, I was living in the refined atmosphere of the books and the learning of the ages. Others worked, and I nourished my mind through years of delightful companionship. Surely I am under a bond for the rest of my life to be efficient in human service, beyond the thousand others who had never one-tenth part of my golden opportunities. God put me to shame well deserved, if I ever sit down content still to draw on the toilers of the earth for my living, and do not try to give back what my education has cost. My education is as sacred a thing as the water purchased by men's blood at the well of Bethlehem.

Suppose, on the other hand, the case of the poor man, whose wife and children go scant of bare comforts that he may have his little luxury of tobacco or beer. Suppose, then, that, taking his luxury, he is a worse man and not a better. Suppose that he is surly, self-willed, domineering, and selfish. What right has he to a morsel of luxury that is not turned over into making him a more affectionate and generous husband and father? What good is there in his luxury, if, after it is consumed, he is less of a man, less efficient and less human, than if he had let it alone?

A practical working test is established at once whereby barbarous or injurious luxury is distinguished and cut off.

What article, if any, among our possessions is produced under such conditions as to prostitute human labor? What luxury, if any, do we demand which hurts the character of men to supply? Are there entertainments, the real result of which is to make those who participate in them worse men and women? Are there costly habits which almost of necessity tend to greed or sensuality? Will good women wear plumage, every dollar of the cost of which is the price of the destruction of beautiful birds, and the hardening of the hearts of the boys and men who murder them? What if the social use of wine has come to mean a vast annual deterioration of the manhood of a people? What shall we judge of the luxury the use of which involves the ruined homes of many thousand sorrowful wives and children? Or, again, are people really civilized whose approval makes the demand for the ballet at the theatre? Is it good for any girls to devote their lives to a kind of dance which most of those who witness would think it shameful for their own girls to practise? Whatever the answer to these questions, all must agree that we have no right to any luxury, the use of which on the whole results in the lowering of the manhood or womanhood of those who provide or indulge in it.

The law of efficiency holds even with the invalids and the aged. You send the sick friend your delicacies; you surround her bed with comforts and tender care; you bid physicians and nurses to wait upon her. It is a call to her honor and her love, first, to summon all the life in her to get well if she can, to cease from making this heavy draught needful upon the costly hospital stores of the world; but next, if recovery is hopeless, every friendly attention, every dish of rare fruit, every vase of roses, is a new call to be brave and cheerful to the last breath, and not to let her pain fall as a weight on the hearts of her friends. Thus luxuries are translated into the efficient terms of faith, hope, and love.

We get here a word of illumination about the use of the great city churches, their rich and beautiful music, their lavish scale of expense. Shall we rule these things out as unsuitable to the spirit of religion? Shall we bid men worship in bare upper rooms and build no more church organs? We answer with no negative word. We simply say that the magnificent churches impose a corresponding and tremendous obligation upon those who enjoy them. The more harmonious the service, the more noble the worship, the more persuasive and tender the gospel preached, so much the more commanding is the bond upon the men and women who enjoy the beauty and inspiration of a faith that kings and prophets only dimly saw in their dreams, to go forth to do the deeds and speak the words fitting such a religion. Whereas men once suffered and went to the stake for their religion, they now make their worship the occasion for an hour of luxurious delight. God save them if they do not straightway turn over this costly delight, God-given, into efficient and loving service of humanity! So far as they cannot or will not do this, the name of their churches obviously becomes a shame and a mockery.

Mr. Kipling in his *Jungle Book* has an admirable story, "Rikki-Tikki-Tavi," that illustrates the relation of luxury to efficiency. The little mongoose is exceedingly fond of dainties, bananas, meat, and eggs; neither has he any conscience against eating them. He has just distinguished himself in his master's house by killing a dangerous snake. The family wish to reward

him with all the good things from the dinner-table.
But the mongoose has still serious duties before him.
There are other snakes to be killed immediately; he
must therefore for the present starve himself, and so
keep a clear head for his work. Animal that he is, he
refuses to touch his master's dainties. The story shows
what real self-restraint is. It is not a merely negative
thing; it is not useless denial of self. It has a positive
purpose. There is always a question of reaching the
highest human efficiency. Who has not enough of the
feeling of the athlete, not to say "the spirit of Christ,"
to appreciate this? If our luxury threatens to cut
down our working power, if it spoils the balance of
nerves or brain, if it saps the moral judgment, if it thus
makes beasts or slaves of us, we remember how Mr.
Kipling's excellent little mongoose would not taste a
dainty morsel of food till his work was accomplished;
and his superb self-control saved all the lives in the
household.

V.

LUXURY AND THE COMMON WEALTH.   We ought now to agree that luxuries are
good to share, to distribute, to spread abroad.
In this view luxuries may take on a wholesome and ennobling significance. The great question
now is, how can our luxuries be lifted out of the selfish,
egotistic, and barbaric level to the new thought of a
common wealth? To co-operate efficiently in work is to
become civilized. To share also as widely as possible
in the results of the common labor is the fulfilment
of civilization. It is a characteristic of barbaric luxury
that its narrow use ministers to egotism and pride. Its
enjoyment marks its possessor as separate from others.

A private park, a grand retinue of needless servants, or
the wearing of costly and conspicuous jewellery, is an
example of such uncivilized luxury. The very intent is
to establish a special privilege or a monopoly from
which the many are shut off. It is the pleasure of the
half-civilized mind to be exclusive.

This is the nature of all ostentatious display, of lavish
self-indulgence, of extravagant feasting. The luxuries
of the beneficent, on the contrary, never separate their
fortunate possessors from the common life of mankind.
The intent of enlightened men is that their pleasures
shall be extended to the largest possible number. They
do not wish to be exclusive in their enjoyment. They
would like to have all enabled to enter into the same
kind of pleasure. What inhumanity to desire anything
else! In their hands, therefore, the same luxury that,
used only for egotism, bars its owner apart, and breeds
envy in the hearts of the needy beholders, becomes a
means to enrich many lives, and to bind men together in
sympathy.

Thus it has been the special function of wealth to
foster art, literature, and music. There are no luxuries
more ennobling than beautiful pictures. There are few
delights greater than exquisite and costly music. In
these, the purest of all luxuries, is an almost endless ca-
pacity for the sharing and extending of delight. It is not
merely stupid waste and shame to buy the rare painting
and lock it up in one's own private gallery, but it is a
sort of robbery not to share the delight of the beautiful
thing with the thousands for whose sake, like a work
of nature, the good God had inspired it. Wealth has so
far been slow and dull in realizing its opportunities in
this direction. It is beginning to be enlightened enough

to know how to get its money's worth out of its luxuries. Let it build Palaces of Delight for the people alongside of the workshops and factories; let it dot the land with public libraries in every village; let it bring concerts and theatres within reach of the poor; let it erect school-houses and colleges, and establish scholarships; let it throw open beautiful grounds and gardens to the people; let it not venture in selfish exclusiveness to shut off its walks on the shore of the sea, or the glorious views of the hills; let it send its carriages to take the invalids to drive. Wealth is on trial for its good behavior. For every consideration of justice and humanity, the posses-sors of wealth must see to it that they share and dis-tribute as well as enjoy.

VI.

WHAT THE SELFISH HAVE TO SAY.   The foregoing section probably seems plain enough to the larger number of readers. It is perfectly plain to those who have no prop-erty themselves. It is obvious as to the re-sponsibility of other people. It is conclusive to any one who looks at life for a moment from the Christian or humanitarian point of view. We must not forget, however, that up to the present time it has been very uncommon for men to consider wealth from this point of view, except on Sunday, or in books, or with respect to the duties of one's neighbors. The difficulty is in applying this simple doctrine of wealth to one's own case. The Anglo-Saxon mind, through long-established custom, traditions, and law, tends toward a specially tenacious and exclusive sense of private and personal rights over property. Men still need to be converted to see and to realize the splendid and inexorable truth

of our doctrine that wealth and luxury are sacred.
"Have I not a right," we hear men say, "to do what
I please with my own? I inherited my fortune, or I
earned it with my own labor; it is mine. I propose to
spend it in my own way. If I like to wear diamonds,
or to drink choice wines, or to keep my strip of land by
the sea clear of intruders, or to shut up my pictures for
my family and my friends, or to put a lock on my pew-
door, no one has any business to criticise my conduct.
I pay for my luxuries." If men do not say this in
words, they say it often in acts.

One wonders how any intelligent man dares to say
of the whole of his fortune, "This is mine by clear moral
right." The network of industrial relations is too com-
plicated to allow any man to be sure how large a part
of what he legally lays claim to is strictly and fairly
his own. Take the case of inherited wealth. By what
righteous standard does its owner inherit a right to
draw upon the labor of thousands of men, or to eat and
drink at a single feast the net results of many days of
their toil? Men, indeed, once believed that they had a
similar right by inheritance to rule a city or a kingdom.
The world has slowly come to doubt the claim of its
self-made lines of princes, and has found out that their
inheritance of political power is against the true inter-
ests of society. Surely the laws of the inheritance of
money power, whether wise or foolish, exist to-day only
by the good will and consent of the people. There can
be no "natural right" by which the grandson of a slave-
trader, a brewer, a fortunate speculator, the lucky possessor of a farm within the limits of a growing town,
shall hold a perpetual mortgage over the land, the houses
and ships, the wharves, the industrial tools, and even the

steam and electrical power on which the lives of a million men depend.

Suppose, now, the man says, "I earned and saved this property myself." Yes, but by the co-operation of the world. Others labored, discovered, ran dangerous risks, wasted their substance in doubtful experiments, and died poor; martyrs and heroes and patriots, a mighty procession, gave their lives, that civilization might be established, that free men might safely build cities, that a vast framework of laws might bind states together, that the colossal modern system of credit might be erected on the foundations of trust and good faith. Thousands of faithful men — workmen, clerks, machinists, builders, customers — contributed to the rearing of the very fortunes that individuals dare to call their own. Who that knows the rudiments of the history of civilization, who that traces effects to their causes, has the effrontry to look us in the face and say, "I earned my fortune alone"? The very word "fortune" contradicts such an assertion. Fortune presupposes an element beyond any desert.

It is possible, however, that a man's friends, if not the man himself, may claim that he deserves of society more than any amount of money or luxury can ever repay. Who can measure the value of the services of the gifted mind that invents a new industry to set ten thousand pairs of hands at work, or that adds a new or cheapened comfort to the lives of millions? Who can pay Bessemer or Lord Kelvin too much for his rare intelligence? But how does this gifted mind itself arise? Lord Kelvin is himself the fruit of the great tree of humanity. What can he give that he did not also receive, from the labor, the thought, the experience, of centuries, from the stored-up learning of the world, from the co-operation of an army of associates in his work, and, last and most of all, from the inspiration of the informing Mind of the universe, the eternal Wisdom. Let no genius proudly say, " I deserve to ride in my carriage and to lord it over my fellows." Let him modestly acknowledge the truth, " I give what I have received; all I have is the gift of God. ' From God for man.' "

Grant, however, for a moment, all that the most arrogant man might claim. Suppose a Vanderbilt to prove that by his individual contribution of organizing genius he had added a thousand million dollars, ten times his own fortune, to the farms of the United States. Let him prove that no one else would have done this work if he had not lived. Let us say that it is all his to do whatever he pleases with. It is private and personal. He shall write his own name as large as he likes on all his possessions. We will not, for the moment, interpose a query about his absolute legal right. What then? Does the man thus forfeit his manhood? Does he really wish to hold all for himself?

There is a man in a certain home by whose plate every morning is set a little pitcher of cream. He pays the bills of the house, and has a legal right to the cream. He accordingly pours it out for himself, while the others take the skimmed milk. What extremely short word have we to describe the kind of man who does this? The same word characterizes every man whose wealth and legal rights are out of proportion to the size of his soul. It describes the thoughtless and greedy people who consume the cream of the products of the world, careless how their brothers live. It describes those of the educated class who imagine that education is for private culture, and not to make men and women wiser trustees, ministers and helpers for the enrichment and uplifting of their less fortunate brothers.

No! There is simply one thought that saves the use of luxuries from narrowing the natures and corrupting the lives of those who possess them. It is the recognition of a sacred quality in every item of those extra enjoyments, of which there is not enough as yet for all equally to share. Nay, rather it is the recognition of a sacred element in all human life. We are not our own, to do as we please with our lives. We are not mere individuals, like forest trees, to grow as large as each one can, reckless of the fate of the rest. We belong in a social world; we are bound together for common weal or woe. We cannot prosper by ourselves, unless we help all to prosper. Indeed, we draw all our life from a common source; we belong to a divine universe. We are here to work out the purpose of that universe. The only conceivable purpose is Beneficence. All our wealth and luxury is for that purpose, or else it is vain. We cannot use our luxury, then, except in the spirit of beneficence, without spoiling it. This is the inexorable law of life. The proclamation of it is the witness that we are the children of God. God lives in love. We cannot therefore live otherwise.

VII.

WHAT ALL MEN WANT: PURE JOY AND DELIGHT.   It may be that some one may already have put in an important interrogation mark. Is not this teaching about luxury somewhat hard and utilitarian? Is it true that, besides all the tedious work of the world, our luxuries must also be translated into terms of efficiency, or even philanthropy ? Cannot we ever be let alone, without being reminded that we are here to do good ? In short, is there not a valid element of pure joy in life ? And are not luxuries really involved with this necessity in man's soul for free and pure joy and delight ?

We have been coming all the way to this point. The great function of luxury doubtless is in the production of joy. It is not enough that the house merely gives shelter; it is well that its ample room adds a sense of freedom and gladness. It is not enough that the great public building stands like a huge box, full of offices or schoolrooms; it is also well that the beauty of its proportions and its architectural adornments shall give delight to the eyes of men for generations. It is not enough that the table-fare shall provide a sufficient number of grains of protein and the other foods, as if for convicts in prison. Man craves the gladsome sense of variety and plenty; he likes beautiful glass and china and silver; he craves pleasant companionship at his table; his æsthetic nature wants the material for delight and development. Pictures and statues, the countless modes of decoration in furnishing and dress, are not for use, but for joy. Music, too, is largely for pure joy; so is the drama. The same element is in literature. It is not enough to teach, to describe, to communicate facts; form, style, order, unity, it may be also poetic fancy, rhythm, and rhyme, must contribute joy to the mind that reads the story or contemplates the facts. How large a part of all the labor of the world goes to make joy! What unthanked months and years of toilsome practice go on, out of sight, in order to make the delight of a single entertainment, a grand concert, a Queen's Jubilee, a World's Fair!

This is so true that we have a new test and critique by which to distinguish between legitimate luxury and the false, extravagant, and wasteful kinds. The wholesome luxury produces pure joy, like new life, not to be measured. Grant that the thing of beauty, the picture or statue, costs a lifetime of toil. It is well, if the sight of it gives men a thrill of infinite delight. Grant that the grand pageant — the World's Exposition — demanded millions of money. But it is still a dream of gladness to thousands who made sacrifice to look on its white palaces. Grant that the alabaster box of ointment seemed too much for one woman to give. But no ointment ever distributed its perfume so far and so long.

We know the vicious or useless luxury, on the other hand, by its failure to make joy. It even smothers joy. The pampered child, surfeited with sweets, surrounded with toys, tended by obsequious servants, does not get joy enough; he is bored and wearied. The laborer's children in the cottage laugh more gayly. The rich lady, with her great expensive household, with her gowns and jewels, with books and art treasures, crowding upon her, with the continents and the seas open to her, misses true joy. Excessive or ill-used luxury breeds worriments. The luxurious class naturally furnishes the pessimists, restless, unhappy, foreboding trouble, contemplating suicide. No class of humble workers furnishes so many pessimists.

There is a rigorous law of proportions about these things. Joy is an element of life, as much as nitrogen is an element in the body; but you cannot force joy and build up life with the materials of joy alone, any better than you can build up the body with a single element. As Browning aptly says of the man who has got truth,

but no heart or will to balance his truth, so we may say
of the man who has luxury without intelligence, sympathy, and good-will to correspond, —

> "The lamp o'erswims with oil, the stomach flags
> Loaded with nurture, and that man's soul dies."

All legitimate luxury, then, is for the sake of man's joy.
It is in order to deepen the flow of the joy that we are
bound to understand, use, and control our luxuries.

The element of joy is not in man alone. It is everywhere abroad in the world, it is in nature, it is in the
life of God. The sparkle of the waves in the summer
breeze, the multitudinous patterns of the frost-work, the
songs of the birds, the gay colors of the wings of the
butterflies, the play of the young lambs, the racing,
gambolling porpoises, even the twinkling stars, bring to
our minds, along with the undertone of mystery and
majesty in the encompassing nature, the sense of pure joy
and mirth, never far away from the heart of the great
creative Power. We think of pain as bound up with
some deep necessity; it is the cost of life; it is that
which life is set to overcome. Life grows nobler in the
task of overcoming it and changing it to good. But the
joy of the world seems to be because God loves joy;
it is the voice of the victorious Love, becoming sweeter
and freer with each age of enlarging life.

VIII.

JOY AND HUMAN EFFICIENCY. Did we agree that pure joy is an end in
itself? Did we deny the bare utilitarian
doctrine that everything must be viewed
with reference to economy and efficiency? The truth
is, that the test of a man's success is not merely in what

he can do, not even in the sum of social good that he can accomplish. The supreme test of the man is in the amount and fulness of his manhood. You can never separate the things that "God hath joined together." Utility, beauty, goodness, manhood, all are one. Utility and duty are only different aspects of the underlying unity. In a high and true sense, therefore, joy always marches with efficiency. Make a man happy, and, other things being equal, he will do more work in a day. Make the child glad in his school, and he gets his lessons quicker. Surely there is no waste in the energy that sings at its work.

It is strange that every intelligent employer does not see this wonderful relation between happiness and efficiency. Does any one dream that a force of discontented men will ever be profitable by the side of joyous workmen? Joyless wage-labor is wasteful precisely as slave-labor was wasteful. You must make even your cattle comfortable in order to get the most out of them; you must make men more than comfortable,— you must make them happy. But see here the subtle law. You can succeed in making cattle comfortable, for the sake of your selfishness, to get the most profit out of them; you never can make men happy so. The one thing that will make the man happy is to respect his manhood, to treat him with frankness, complete justice, and sympathy, to give him your heart; in short, to keep the Golden Rule toward him. The business world, always pressing toward higher modes of efficiency, is already beginning to catch the secret of this divine unity of plan. Only civilized men, that is, complete men, with all the elements of their manhood nourished and satisfied, can do the work of a civilized world.

Utility or efficiency is thus everywhere one with joy. But joy is the higher aspect; it represents that out of which energy itself proceeds. In other words, it is fulness of life. For who is our model and perfect athlete? He is not surely the man with narrow margin of strength, nervous and anxious, who faints away as he touches the prize; but he is the man who, running with all his might, seems to draw on an inexhaustible reserve, and wears on his face the confidence and hope of a victor. So the true master of the secret of life is not only faithful unto death, but also bears in his heart the freedom, the joy, and the hope befitting God's sons. Is there anything in which God can more truly be conceived to rejoice than in this superbundance of life?

IX.

THE QUES-
TION OF
SORROW
AND PAIN.
The fact faces us still that we are in a world where sorrow, disappointment, and death are. The poor are always with us; the mourners go about the street; tragedies of injustice are enacted. War still desolates the fair earth. The ascetic and Puritan impulse is in us to repudiate joy in such a world. How can we have human sympathies, and be glad, while multitudes suffer? What right have we to lift up joyous faces and sing in the very presence of those who weep? There are moods in which these questions seem unanswerable. In other words, there are times in which we must simply yield to our sympathies, and "weep with those who weep." Alas for any soul that never is touched by the cry of "human toil and crime."

Grant now, what we have already suggested, that we have a use for every note, up and down the scale, whereby the mystery of man's life is interpreted. There are three tremendous considerations that forbid us from allowing the music of the world to be prevailingly written in the minor key. In the first place, there is the central thought of God. Let a man be an utter agnostic, and yet, if he is intelligent, the mighty " Perhaps," the sublime possibility that the long procession of the prophets and saints have been right, at least in the direction of their march, must sometimes thrill the human mind with joyous wonder. Let a man believe ever so faintly in truth, in beauty, in order, in unity, in the ideal things; let him merely purpose to conduct his life on that side as against chaos, untruth, unfaithfulness; let him only once in a while catch the light of the stars, — and he can not help being glad, as when the summer sun shines before his face. In short, as Paul says, " if God be for us," in any real sense of the word, " who can be against us ? " Or, what can " separate us from the love of God " ? Why, then, we ask, should " children of the King go mourning all their days " ?

Again, we rightly grieve over the sorrows of the poor. Pray God we may never forget the oppressed races. Let us not be so dull, however, as to suppose that the poor do nothing but starve, or that the oppressed nations suffer a monotone of despair. The sunlight and the starlight, nameless human kindnesses and heroisms, and the presence of God, are with the poor and oppressed, as truly as with the rich and the powerful. The children of the poor are as near to God's heart in their simple mirth as other children are. When was it ever discovered that joy depended on many possessions ? Everywhere, even in the very teeth of armed violence, love stories are enacted; in war as in peace young men and maidens are married and given in marriage. Every-where in the cabins of peasants and serfs, babies' faces carry the pure joy of God to mothers' hearts. The sick have their hours of refreshment. The standing wonder of the world is that human nature, like some divine thing, turns tears and blood and pain into new forms of life. The wonder is, in reading the story of the oppressed nations, that oppression has never permanently quelled the invincible spirit of liberty and manhood. In the long struggle upward from barbarism and in the darkest ages, hope that somewhere all would yet be well has animated the hearts of myriads of brave sufferers. We pitied the blacks in their bondage, but the blacks did not despair. On every plantation in the Christmas-time men saw the joyous merry-makings of the slaves. If the slave and the poor and the sick can rejoice, shall we not all rejoice too? It is the common human nature that draws us closer together. We will not relax one effort for relief, because our hearts have throbbed together in joy, as well as in sorrow.

Moreover, we wish to know how best to help our suffer-ing brethren. Shall we do them any good by trying to carry the woe of the world on our shoulders? Will it help any one to be freer of poverty or sorrow or oppres-sion, if we act as if there were no good God in the uni-verse? Let us go to the very poor, and ask them what they want of those who chance to be better off than they are. We have already seen that the poor are probably only too fond of the splendor and pomp of the luxu-rious class. The poor tend to encourage lavish display. They desire to see more, not less, of the joy and glory of life. Men are like children in this respect. Even in the eyes of the jaded and forlorn, the joy of the thoughtless and selfish is better than sadness and monotony. The great, gay, splendid city, with its two terrible extremes, is nevertheless richer in the resources that constitute life than a barren level of communal uniformity. The poor would not thank the rich to strip away their bright plumage, and to shut up the doors at Delmonico's and Tiffany's. They demand rather that the rich shall behave worthily of their grand responsibilities; they ask the rich not to destroy the precious material for making joy, but to show how more chances may be open to themselves and their children to win the same. Everywhere the voice of the poor to the more prosperous is not to forbid joy, but to do justice, to "lend a hand," to help all to share the common heritage of joy, in which all men surely ought to have a part.

Let us go to the hospitals, where pain and suffering are massed together, and let us make the patients tell us whom they wish to see in their wards. Do they wish to see sorrowful faces and tears? The very reverse. They want joy and hope quite as much as sympathy. They want nurses and visitors who bring smiles and cheerful words; they like to hear the voices of happy children. Come and sing beautiful songs to them. Tell them of the good things that you know, of other sick ones who are recovering; tell them about the gayety and the flowers at the last wedding or party. They will not thank you for dwelling on their sufferings. Yes, when they may be feeling the worst, show them the faces of men and women shining with the light of their faith in God.

We will put the same kind of question to those who sorrow for the death of their friends. Shall we dress in crape? Shall we shut out the sunshine from our houses? Shall the marriage-bells be stopped? Shall the children's play be hushed? No. There is no sad heart that does not crave light and joy. The cure of melancholy is in the children's gladness. The weeds of mourning are the survival of bygone superstitions; the darkened windows are a barrier to the influx of the life of God. Face about toward the light; let no sorrow of yours needlessly weight down the shoulders of toiling men; work on, hope on. Here is the gospel that forever turns sorrow into ampler and deeper life. You will help sorrowing friends by such sympathy alone as carries love, hope, and gladness.

We have here a word to all sad-eyed reformers. What sort of men does the world demand to do its costly work of regeneration? It wants the same kind of men that it asks for its physicians and surgeons. However much you respect frank truthfulness, you want no pessimist for your physician; neither do you want any one to cry over your suffering. You summon to your need the kind of physician who is always hoping for the best. The true physician should be a whole man; he should possess faith as well as charity. In some simple form he should be a believer in God. Such a man carries an atmosphere of health, gladness, and life. The world wants the same sort of large-natured men for its moral, social, and political reformers. Why is it, when the teacher has long since given up the rod, that the reformer should still hold it over the back of the world, and think to drive and frighten men into the way of goodness? The jeremiads, the maledictory psalms, the old-time denunciations of the wicked, should be stored in the museums with the bows and arrows of the primeval men. Even the capitalists and the politicians are men like ourselves, to be approached, therefore, with the

tone of those who speak a gospel. Why should reform
be made to appear a bitter pill to be forced down men's
throats? Why should not the most chronic and refrac-
tory patient be made glad that there is a way of rescue
and new life?

X.

SACRIFICE IN SUCH SENSE THAT CHILDREN WOULD DESIRE IT. We have agreed that there is a sacred quality in all luxury. We have seen that in this thought is the clew to the wise, safe, and humane treatment of all the means, resources, and appurtenances of joyous life. We are ready to carry this thought now to its logical conclu-
sion, and to annex the whole golden region of joy and
pleasure to the republic of our common humanity. We
will set pure joy where it belongs, — under the unity of
religion.

We may draw a profound lesson here, by way of illustration, from the ancient superstitions. The primitive
man looked upon all exceptional good fortune — success in
the chase, the discovery of water in the desert, the birth
of a son and heir, the finding of treasure, a bounteous
harvest — as a gift of the gods. Woe unto the man who
in his pride ventured to take his good luck as his own, and
without thought of the invisible powers that surrounded
him! The great feast must be made sacred by prayers,
libations, and offerings. The treasure must be made to
pay tribute to the temples. Victory was celebrated with
the payment of vows. The custom of "saying grace"
at table is the survival of this ancient sentiment; it
comes down from the hungry times, when the gift of
plenty seemed an almost miraculous boon. The idea
was that men ate in the presence of their god; they took

his gifts in reverence. It was as if he bade them eat and drink in his name. His worshippers were not their own masters, eager to eat, like wild beasts, before the mighty unseen Host gave the word.

The solemn marriage rites of all nations convey the same idea. Beauty, joy, and love were the gifts of the gods. Man might not touch them unbidden. It was for him to wait reverently, in due regard for their sacred character, till the word of permission came from above. Then the sanction of the invisible world was added to love, and made a perpetual defence about the new home. The voice of the god, above the voices of all the guests, bade the husband and wife to love and be thankful, to be reverent evermore, and the more to rejoice.

Under ceremonial, superstition, and priestcraft a great and universal idea was working to consciousness. We are able now to translate it into the simplest and most rational terms. There is not only force at the secret heart of things, and force dominant in nature swinging the planets; there is not only law and order compelling all changing phenomena to take on form, pattern, and beauty; there is not only thought or mind shining everywhere; there is not only an irresistible spirit of the universe swaying man's soul, as if by an inward voice urging him to follow right " in the scorn of consequence," stirring him by splendid visions and ideals to take the hitherto untrodden way of truth — there is also in the central and encompassing life what we men call love; it seeks not obedience merely, but welfare, not only efficiency of accomplishment, as of ingenious machines, but divine delight and satisfaction. The idea of the old-time blessing at the daily meal is forever true. The

Eternal bids his children eat and drink and be merry. Let them be reverent, obedient, humble, gentle, beneficent, and so much the fuller will be their pure joy. The old-time puritan custom of family prayers, rightly understood, carried a deep and rational significance. Each day belonged to God; each life went forth on a divine mission. The cares of the day and its joys alike belonged to the eternal and universal order; nothing human was outside this order. The wedding ceremony still tells us modern men the same story. It lifts wedded love into an eternal relationship. It is not a private and personal love; it is a revelation of the love of God.

We have come now to a definite understanding of that much abused and misunderstood word *sacrifice.* It has been often supposed that to sacrifice anything was to give it away, forswear or renounce it. The real, as well as the literal, meaning is to make a thing sacred. You lift it out of the narrow, animal, material, or selfish level into the higher, divine, and universal order. You lift the single stone, worthless and insignificant by itself, into the wall of the temple of humanity. To make the thing sacred is to make it, like all God's work, beneficent. To consecrate a thing, to make it "holy," is thus to constitute it a part of the unity of God's world. This is creative work. Man is herein taken into God's confidence, as it were, and allowed to co-operate in his thought.

Apply this idea of sacrifice now to man's joy and luxury. Joy and sacrifice have been thought incompatible. To make a sacrifice was to forswear joy. To be religious was to narrow life, and to cut off a part of its income. The true thought is the very reverse. It is to conceive of the joy as from God; it is to enter into a higher and larger meaning of joy; it is to hold the joy as one holds any sacred trust. So far from hindering the flow of joyous feeling, we have all obstruction of fear and doubt taken away when, as Tennyson says, the sweeter inward voice cries, " Rejoice, rejoice!" Alas for a man when the joy is of such a kind that it cannot be made sacred. For then the sense of unrest and restraint either stifles the soul, or turns the abandon of pleasure into a consuming madness.

As with joy, so with sorrow, the new or higher thought of sacrifice takes the soul out of its isolation, loneliness, and egotism. To make a thing sacred is to say of it that God is with us in it. He is with us in our joy; he is also our companion in loss or grief. We are not alone; we are citizens of the universe; "our times are in his hands;" if he is in our joy, we may reverently say that our sorrow enters also into his life. And this is the source of a deeper joy.

Does any one object that this is too wonderful and good to believe? But this would be practically to say that it is too wonderful for us to believe in God! The truth is, that we are as yet only on the verge of understanding what it means, when we call ourselves, after Jesus' fashion, "the children of God." Does any one still draw back from so tremendous and logical a faith as this? But curiously enough, the conception of a universe without God is even more wonderful and incredible. It is a conception that translates the whole stately frame of the universe into insignificance, impotence, and death. Whereas, the religious conception that frankly places all souls in the presence of victorious Beneficence, translates everything, both in theory and practice, upwards into power, peace, gladness, and life, — the very things that all men are made by nature to seek. Let us make this perfectly plain.

XI.

THE GOOD LIFE AS A SACRAMENT.   The old, base, and animal tendency is to take and use joy as if man had only himself to think of. It is unconscious atheism. The story of King Nebuchadnezzar's boast, "Is not this great Babylon which I have built?" is the classic object-lesson of egotistic pride in one's own possessions. The favorite words of this kind of pride are "I" and "mine." The animal propensity is to hoard up for one's self the resources of life. The vain and small soul looks back and dwells on its own winnings as it broods over its petty losses. The story of the manna in the wilderness is a parable to illustrate this way of regarding life. The manna was good while it was fresh; but the story was, it turned to corruption as soon as one tried to keep it over night. So with joy; so with life. It is good day by day, fresh as it comes. But no man can store it away for himself. Hoard it up, try to put your private mark upon it, and it always eludes you; it turns into anxieties, apprehensions, vanity, stinginess, disappointment. Like Nebuchadnezzar, the self-centred and irresponsible despots go crazy; the selfish lovers lose the prize of love; the luxurious grow obese and die. The little child, like the birds, may take his life fresh from the hand of God every morning without asking what it is for; but when man has once asked the man's question what life means, he must henceforth lay joy altogether on the altar of sacrifice. An inexorable but beneficent law drives him on the venturesome way of his growth as a son of God.

The sacrifice of life, as we have seen, is the making of life sacred or holy. The new or Christian conception of life is that it belongs unreservedly to God, that is, to Beneficence. Life is a trust for love's sake. To make life sacred means to turn it to the highest ends, to admit no element into it that is not beneficent. In other words, we devote life in all its motions to the social good. This is to make life sacred.

High up among the hills flows the great glacial stream from the melting snows, the inexhaustible resources of heaven. Down below on the arid plain the stream comes to us. Through each man's little farm runs the channel of the blessed invigorating waters. Every drop of the water is sacred to Beauty and Use, to make flowers grow, to raise good crops of corn and fruit, to leap from fountains and dance in the sunshine, to cool the lips of cattle and men. Use it, enjoy it, let each make his little farm green with its pure flow; let no one obstruct or waste it as it runs on to other farms down the valley. So life flows to every soul of us from the fountains of God. Every moment of it likewise is sacred to Beauty, to Truth, to Duty, to Love.

We may illustrate and apply our thought in certain familiar instances. Take, for example, the Thanksgiving feast or the birthday celebration. We may say in all reverence that the Almighty bids us take the festivity, the music, the flowers, the congratulations of friends, as so many signs of the Eternal Goodness. But all this high joy is ours as a trust. We cannot narrowly say "I" and "mine" about it. We have no right to keep it to ourselves. What splendid word comes after the music has come and the friends have departed? It is somewhat like this: God make me more generous all the days of my life for the sake of this rich joy. God keep me humble, gentle, helpful, and turn this joy of mine into the stream of the world's joy, so as to deepen its flow. Such is the grand religious spirit of sacrifice, that lets no life be lived for itself.

We will suppose that some young girl has the charm of grace and beauty. What shall she do? Shall she hide her beauty behind a veil, or go into a convent? Shall she mortify her bright young spirit with coarse and unbeautiful dress? Shall she try to deny the fact of her beauty? No! Let her be very glad and thankful for her joy-compelling gifts. The world needs grace and beauty. Let her therefore hold these gifts sacred. This does not mean to spoil and ignore them. It means to recognize the truth that they came from God; it means that she will never turn them over to the uses of vanity, pride, and selfishness; it means that she will be glad in them for love's sake, as one would be glad to give a drink of cold water to the thirsty. The girl's beauty is not her own to please herself with; it is a trust wherewith she shall add the charm of her life to the beneficent purpose of God. Can any one doubt for a moment that beauty, thus turned over into the terms of noble sacrifice, becomes richer and sweeter for all souls that look upon it? Can any one doubt that, thus lifted up into the plane of our common humanity and held sacred there, beauty passes into the spiritual realm and becomes eternal? The very secret of beauty, in fact, is that it is the visible emblem of love.

We will suppose, again, some young man of large and exceptional endowments. He has health, energy, manly virtue, good sense and good temper, intellect and wit, all crowned with a truly liberal education. Shall we ask him to make a sacrifice of all that he has? Yes, we can ask nothing less than the nation ·asked of Lincoln, or than the world asked of Jesus. We bid him put his splendid endowments to the highest and most effective use for the service of man. We beg him never to imagine that he created this fine equipment, or that he holds it for himself. It is the most sacred of trusts. It is for this splendid reason that we bid him also be heartily and reverently glad of his gifts. It is as if the Almighty had made over to him a rare and wonderful instrument, or some new force, and had charged him to put this instrument or this new force to the utmost use for the benefit of humanity. What should we think, if, charged with such a purpose, he turned his power to the growth of his own conceit, selfishness, and egotism, or even to the oppression of the very men whom he was set to minister unto? Must we not say that to hold any power sacred is the most reasonable use of that power? Does any one begin to understand what power is, or what it is for, until he looks upon it as a social trust? Is a man, indeed, fully a man, till he conceives of himself as simply a son of God, the citizen of a universe, not therefore his own master, but the minister of the forces of God?

Take another instance. Let us suppose that a man has achieved some great success. He has organized a new industry; he has discovered a new element; he has established a principle; he has painted a picture; or he has made a poem that the world will read for ages after he is gone. What shall we say about his success? We say, let him be both utterly humble and unreservedly happy in his success. If he has been the voice through which the message of God has come into the world, if he has adjusted the wires over which fresh access of power and life has come, why should he not be glad? Let him see to it now that his success be turned into fresh power and service. What else was his success but the life of the universe, surging up in the fortunate moment into victory? Others before him had labored, and he had harvested the fruits of their labor. His success is not his own; it is sacred. It shall forbid him to be arrogant; it shall bind him over to be forever generous, gentle, affectionate, simple-hearted. God forbid that the man ever should go about the street sad and forlorn, who has been permitted to do a good and helpful thing for humanity! Shall he demand reward or payment? Was it not joy enough to do the deed?

We cannot make the true and higher meaning of sacrifice too clear. Let us take another instance. We will suppose that some one has won the great prize of love; the eyes of a true and generous wife have watched over his welfare; he has tasted the sweetness of a happy home; children have come to brighten his life; the friendship of good men and gracious women has blessed and enriched him. All these munificent gifts are sacred; they are not merely private and personal, but they spring out of the life of the universe. The soul that has known pure love has been made a divine trustee for love's sake. He cannot henceforth say " I " and " mine " about love. He cannot hoard his treasure; even if death comes to his loved ones, he cannot brood over his loss. God forbid that any man upon whose face the eternal light has shone, into whose heart the priceless and infinite gift of love has descended, should ever be heartbroken! God forbid that he should forget what he has had, or lose his splendid memories, or, having known love, that he should not henceforth know both faith and hope.　For all love is sacred; whoever has known love has come under a bond to show forth love forever.

XII.

THE LAW OF JOY.　We now read out from all our experiences a profound law of life.　The law of man's life is to march erect, with his face to the front.　To look backward, to live regretful over the past, to contemplate its disappointments and reverses, and to stay in the evil company of one's mistakes and sins, is to thwart and spoil life.　If a man were his own master, he might have a right thus to live in the past, to beat his breast as much as he pleased, to shut himself up in the grim castle of his egotism.　The truth is, he is not his own master.　He is like a soldier under orders to hasten forward.　Lame, wounded, beaten, blinded, he is still in the service; he must add his little to the help of the rest.　While life lasts, it is all for the sake of the great cause.

Pleasure and personal success become therefore incidental.　The man's work is larger than to get pleasure or success for himself.　His work is to put his whole life out in the service of the Beneficent Powers.　He may seem, like William the Silent, never to win success in his immediate undertakings.　It is enough that God's life flows in him.　If God's life is his, joy is his too. He takes it as the soldier takes his rations, his rest, or his furlough, or, on occasion, the tremendous ventures of battle.　"March on," is the voice of the Master. Trust him for more joy and new life as you go.　Real life is here and now; it meets you as you move on.　As Browning says, —

" Was it for mere fool's play, make-believe and mumming,
   So we battled it like men, not boylike, sulked or whined?
Each of us heard clang God's 'Come !' and each was coming:
   Soldiers all, to forward-face, not sneaks to lag behind!

How of the field's fortune? That concerned our Leader!
   Led, we struck our stroke nor cared for doings left and right:
Each as on his sole head, failer or succeeder,
   Lay the blame or lit the praise: no care for cowards: fight! "

We may express the same idea in another form.
What is the law of every little artery and vein in the
body? It is to pass on the flow of the blood. Woe to
the vein that thinks to stop the life, and take it all for
itself. But as the veins each give full and free flow
through themselves, lo! thus they have perfect nourish-
ment. So with the life of man. Let him keep to himself, if he can, the good that comes to him, let him be
selfish with it, and presently what seemed good turns to
mischief. Let him now open wide all the valves of his
life; let him take and give all that he gets; let him
pour out the full stream of life, as if all that he had to
do was to enrich others beyond him. His own life, in
this constant and unremitting circulation, thus gets for
itself all that it needs. Stop the circulation for a moment, and disease begins to set in. Clear away obstruction, remove friction, increase the flow of the life, and
disease disappears as if by magic. Every form of life
is thus seen to be a kind of trust. It is not our own,
it is universal; it is sacred, as from God. To sacrifice
life, as Jesus taught, is not to lose, but to understand
and gain life eternal.

XIII.

MAN'S MOST PERMANENT INVEST-MENTS. We ought by this time to have taken the word "sacrifice" entirely out of the class of dreadful and negative things, and to have placed it forever, where it belongs, among the great positive and inspiring watchwords. What every chivalrous soul really wants is the opportunity of sacrifice, in other words, the opportunity of growth and life. Jesus expressed this fact when he said that the kingdom of God was "like unto a merchantman seeking goodly pearls, who, when he had found the pearl of great price, went and sold all that he had, and bought it." What should we say if this man began to tell us of the terrible loss that he had undergone! The fact is, the man was never so rich before. His sacrifice was simply the process of translation from lower values into higher and more precious terms.

The child gives up his own way to obey his mother; in that act he grows toward manhood. The youth gives up time and money to secure an education. It is not loss, but wise investment. The bridegroom says, "With all my worldly goods I thee endow;" the words of seeming renunciation are the fulfilment of all the lover's hopes. The mother forgets herself in her children; Nathan Hale, the patriot boy, gives his life. John Bright, the stalwart English reformer, with his young wife lying dead in his house, puts away his own personal sorrow at the thought of the needs of the poor, to do immediate public service for his country. You do not altogether pity the suffering mother, the martyred patriot, the burdened statesman and reformer.

You glory in them; all men are richer for them; they opened the way for more life to come into the world. The hope of immortality itself stands in such lives.

There is no difficulty now in understanding what has seemed to many one of the most difficult of the stories in the New Testament. It is the story of Jesus' treatment of the rich young man, earnest and lovable, who came asking what he must do to possess eternal life. Jesus' treatment of him seems almost harsh. Why should a man who had kept all the laws fail of winning eternal life? The fact is, the young man had not yet caught the idea of what quality "eternal life" is. He knew what a respectable personal life was, but he did not yet see that larger and higher thing, the social and universal life, — the life of God's sons. Eternal life is the life of sacrifice.

We can imagine that some fine young man had come to Washington at Valley Forge with the question, what he needed to do to enter into the life of a patriot. Would Washington have simply told him that he should go on keeping the laws of his country? But the times demanded, as they always demand, something more vital than to keep the laws of decent society. "If you want to be a patriot," we can hear Washington say, "if you wish to be one of my men, do what I am doing; put your fortune and life at risk, come with us, and serve the utmost needs of the people." As a matter of fact, Washington lost neither his life nor his fortune, but he sacrificed them, that is, he held them utterly at the disposal of his country. And we all truly see the gulf of difference between such patriots as Washington and the men at Valley Forge, and men who merely kept the laws, and looked after their property in New York and Philadelphia. So we all see the difference between the rich young ruler and Jesus. It is the world-wide difference between the narrow or selfish life and the social, the universal, the "eternal" life, which holds all things as from God and for man.

XIV.

WHAT EVERY ONE OUGHT TO EXPECT. We rise now to the highest possible doctrine of human efficiency. General Armstrong at Hampton had caught it exactly when he wrote among the noble memoranda that he left after his death, " What is commonly called sacrifice is the best possible use of one's self and one's resources." Is there anything that an intelligent man could more greatly desire than to put his life to its highest possible use ? Is any purer joy possible than to know that one's life goes to make good abound, to make light shine, to add to the sum of human welfare ? If a man could know at every moment that he was where God wanted him, that he was doing at that moment, whether in toil or sorrow, in rest or in friendly intercourse, at the level of his daily tasks or in the height of inspiration, precisely what Beneficence commanded, would not this be the fulness of effective, gladsome living ?

Christianity has hitherto only partially, feebly, and waveringly taught its great doctrine. Christendom has not believed its own gospel. Forsaking the vital religion of Jesus and of all the heroes and saints as impracticable, men have put up with a sort of conventional Christianity, from which the great essential ideas of the **Golden Rule** and the real presence of God were dropped out. We are only beginning to find that these majestic ideas may be trusted and followed to their splendid conclusions, as surely as the law of gravitation or the fact of the sunshine. The fundamental duty of sacrifice is not a sad, repellent, negative rule, to scare the hearts of youth, to minimize life, to check man's eager desire for joy. It is a grand highway, where life may run to its fullest accomplishment and realization. It is a word to stir the chivalry of ardent and noble souls. We cannot repeat to this generation too clearly its stirring gospel — as sure as the universe — that it is safe and beautiful to live as if in the presence of God; that it is safe and beautiful to trust the voices of conscience and love — God's testimony within us; that this is to make all life sacred, to bring life to its highest efficiency.

All details and conditions fall under the one comprehensive law. To sacrifice luxuries is to handle them efficiently for love's sake. How shall they do the most human service? To sacrifice money is to consecrate it to its largest opportunities in making men wise, free, virtuous, happy. To sacrifice time, so far from wasting it, is to spend it in the noblest way. Agassiz and Darwin sacrificed their lives to the discovery of truth. They could not have disposed of their lives in any way so successful or satisfactory. Livingstone and Armstrong, men say, sacrificed their chances for making a fortune. In other words, they gave up a lower and smaller kind of life to take a higher and richer career. Shaw and Winthrop and many another young man in the time of the Civil War died at the outset of their career. Jesus died a young man. Was this loss of life? Did Herod or Caiaphas or Cæsar begin to have life as Jesus enjoyed it? In the eyes of clear intelligence, then, to make a sacrifice is to be doing precisely the thing which is best and most fruitful. To live a life of sacrifice is to be doing at every moment the most useful thing possible; it is to be constantly using the whole of one's power; it is, therefore, to be most alive. What can any man want more and better than this? Is not this the religion for the twentieth century?

XV.

THE DOC-
TRINE THAT
THERE IS
NO EVIL.

Is there no evil, then, some one may ask? Are there not human experiences of which a man may well stand in dread, and cry, "Deliver us from evil"? Are there not crises when the word "sacrifice" seems still to bear exactly the sense of a loss? To these profound questions we must answer both *Yes* and *No*. We do not wish for a moment to blind our eyes to the fact of the tremendous contrasts in the midst of which the life of man goes on as if by rhythmic motion. The law is of alternating darkness and light, summer and winter. It is a cheap philosophy that denies the existence of pain, denies that it has its solemn uses. It is a weak love that would not choose to suffer in the sorrow or the loss of a friend. It is a sentimental and materialistic optimism that cherishes the expectation that we shall banish physical death from the earth. It is a miserable travesty on the old story of the cross that pretends that Jesus ought not really to have felt the touch of the Roman nails in his hands and feet. To the finite sight, looking at things from below, as we make our way upward, there certainly appear narrow and difficult places, the passage through which evermore demands courage, patience, and chivalry. Life at its highest and grandest moments is often an act, not altogether of sight, but of faith. When General Armstrong, looking back over the whole of his life, said that " he never had sacrificed anything," he did not mean that he never had taken any brave ventures; he did not mean that he had never been called to acts that looked at the time to him and to others like sheer waste and loss.

We teach a higher, saner, and sounder philosophy than that pain does not exist, or that the efforts of the heroes cost nothing in overcoming resistance within and without. The majestic teachings of the richest human experience show that all such effort, pain, seeming evil, sacrifice of life, go to the making of manhood, — to "the manifestation of the sons of God." Man must endure the darkness of the night; but around his little earth, while he watches or sleeps, the light plays without ceasing. Let him be glad that it will presently shine again in his face! Man must bear the stress of the storm and the rigor of winter; but God's laws, — let him never forget it, — like the everlasting arms, are underneath him still. The body must waste and die, since every pound of it belongs to the elements of the earth; but its death does not touch the deeper fact of an immortal life, into which, in every moment of real sacrifice, the thinking, loving, willing son of God has entered. Heard from below, the old chivalric call often seems to be to give life away. Looked at from above, even as God sees, as we too see at our best, every sacrifice for Duty, for Truth, or for Love, proves to be gain. To believe this is faith, or religion.

XVI.

THE PARA-
BLE OF
MODERN
INDUSTRY.
   The world is working out a wonderful parable of the higher religion in the industrial order of society. In the old days, to a very large extent, man toiled and hunted and travelled alone. In the Appalachian region of America men still live an extremely isolated life. You will see the solitary traveller pursuing his way over a rough trail on horseback. You will find the little farms where the rude processes of agriculture go on as helplessly as if the whole world were still barbarous. And yet through the midst of men who live in this primitive isolation run the lines of the vast railway system, bespeaking the march of a new order of life. The motto of this new order is co-operation. There is in it the beginning and the prophecy of sacrifice. In combining to build the continental railroads, thousands of scattered men and women have come out of their isolation and narrowness, have parted with their hoarded savings, and have devoted them to a great common and civilizing end. What if they have not altogether seen the true significance of their act? What if they have expected their own gain rather than the gain of a distant community? What if they have been used by the Divine Will for the consummation of his far-reaching purpose? The fact remains that they have been made to join hands, and to contribute for the welfare of mankind. Skilful engineers have drawn on the accumulated knowledge and experience of the centuries; unseen forces have been unlocked from the depths of the earth; in an almost literal sense, the human wagons have been "hitched to a star;" thousands of men may now ride

together and visit one another, where the few once slowly climbed over the hills; the riches of the nation are distributed to meet the needs of each part; new standards of civilized life, new and higher ethics, a more thorough and helpful religion, begin to penetrate into every little hamlet.

XVII.

A CHAL-
LENGE TO
EVERY MAN.
We have called this co-operative indus-trial system which we are building up in the modern world a parable. We are learn-ing in all kinds of outward form to socialize thought, invention, and effort. We find that nothing is for the individual alone. Whatever he gets or holds he must give and share. If he thinks alone, his thought comes to nothing; if he works alone, his work is of the least possible profit; if he invents or discovers anything, he must add it to the common value. If he competes with his fellows, he has to combine with them also. The combinations grow more mighty and intricate. They bind together in more subtle bonds even those who seem to strive as rivals. In short, whatever man does must be lifted up and handed over for the common welfare. No one prospers who does not obey this law. Even the robber and the gambler, who sometimes seem for a little while to thrive in despoiling their fellows, fight hope-lessly against the Almighty. Where on the face of the earth are ill-gotten gains safe? The avenging Nemesis, hardly to be propitiated, follows the man who preys on society. What is the manhood of such a man worth for himself? or what honor will his name bring for his chil-dren?

Throughout the vast realm of industry and business the challenge to every man is, what can you do to meet human needs ? What can you give that man wants ? What can you contribute to the good of mankind ? The exception proves the rule. The quacks, the impostors, the low newspapers, the demagogues, are compelled to meet a human call or desire, even though it be short-lived, morbid, spurious, or childish. The demand creates a supply. The vicious supply can only be supplanted by a nobler and more intelligent demand. In the present half-civilized world, only struggling as yet into the consciousness of its divine destiny, the rule holds, nevertheless, that the world " expects every man to do his duty," that is, to add something to the sum of its life. And the whole industrial system, faulty as it still is, is a parable of the working of this law.

XVIII.

ETERNAL LIFE. Our parable leads us straightway to the great spiritual conception of the meaning of human life. "What is life ? What are we here for ?" asks the child of the mother. Let us be very bold, and say that we are here for sacrifice, and that, too, daily and untiring. Then let us explain to the child that sacrifice is not loss or death, but it is turning everything in this human life into good ; it is making all things sacred, that is, devoting them to good. The life of sacrifice is life lived as if in the presence of God ; it is, therefore, sound, rich, restful, joyous. To stop evil and put good in its place, to spread light, to make love grow, — this is to live like God ; it is to find and to make heaven everywhere.

XIX.

THE DIVINE
FACTORS
OF LIFE.
If we have caught the full meaning of our subject, we must be impressed anew with the fact that the divine life — let us reverently venture to say, the life of God, and therefore the life of his children — is constituted of various elements, not one of which can be dropped or neglected without impairing its goodness. Truth, Mind, the clear Intelligence, is one of these elements that make complete life. Justice, or Righteousness, the stalwart moral sense, is another element. There is pure Joy in life, the delight in Beauty. There is the strain of Sorrow also, ever mysteriously blended with joy, without which sympathy could not be. As the colors of the rainbow, broken apart for the moment and revealed in their separateness, all go together and make the glory of the white sunlight, so all the elements of life blend into the perfect harmony of Love, the infinite Good-will. Mankind is rising to the new consciousness, here and now, of this true and divine life. Every moment of earnest good-will in us reveals it like a flash. Jesus' name stands as the great personal illustration and prophetic object-lesson, — not to show, as men once taught, that this kind of life is hopelessly unique, — but to demonstrate that it is the universal type and order, imperative, therefore, for all the inhabitants of this world, as truly as for any other citizens of this majestic universe in the highest heavens where life may climb.

XX.

THE UNI-
VERSAL
RELIGION.
All the signs of the times point toward "the manifestation of the sons of God." New material conditions, more pressing, complex, and interesting problems, even the strident voices of war, proclaiming that barbarism is still abroad in the earth, add force to the demand. The world is growing tired of a conventional religion of those who say, and do not; it is urging upon schools, universities, churches, and sects its chivalrous call for men and women who, believing in the living God, propose to act accordingly; who, believing in the Golden Rule of Love, propose to make it the sovereign law of their lives. Already, far and near, no longer few, scattered, or depressed, but everywhere learning to find each other out, to hold each other's hands, to lift up their heads in confidence and courage, to win their friends to their faith,

> "There are in this loud, stunning tide
>   Of human care and crime
> With whom the melodies abide
>   Of the everlasting chime;
> Who carry music in their heart
> Through dusty lane and wrangling mart,
> Plying their daily task with busier feet,
> Because their secret souls a holy strain repeat."